RAND, McNALLY & CO.'S
MAP OF THE
Central Portion
OF
CHICAGO.
SHOWING RAILROADS, DEPOTS
AND
STREET TRANSPORTATION LINES.

Explan

Railroads.
Elevated R.R.
Cable Lines
Horse Cars &
Electric Lines

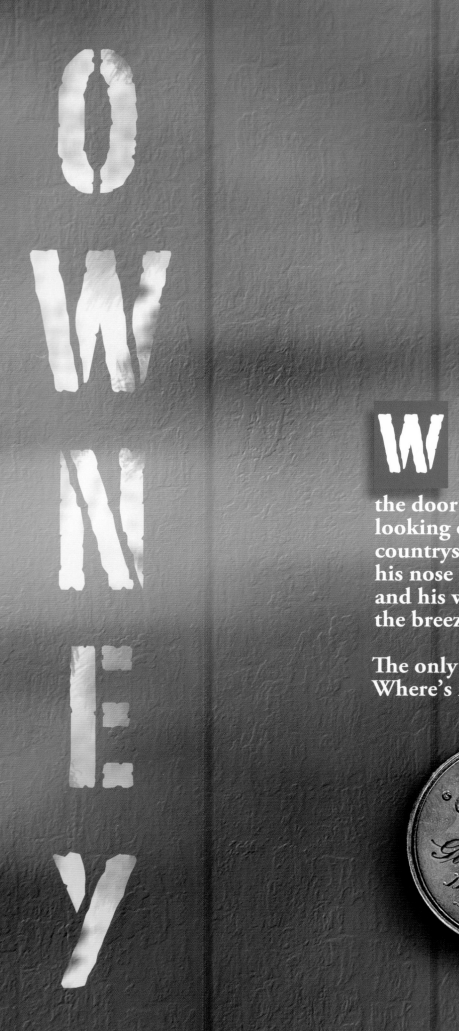

**OWNEY**

**W**hen we think of Owney, we think of what he loves the most--standing in the door of the mail car, looking out at the countryside flying by, his nose filled with scents and his whiskers blowing in the breeze.

The only thing he wonders is Where's next?

**CHICAGO**

As far as Owney is concerned, all adventures begin in Albany. That's his "home station." Yet his heart is also with the people he's met and the places where he has traveled over the years. Today the adventure will be going to Chicago. Owney loves Chicago.

On the train the men work in the moving rail mail cars just like they do back in the Albany building, for each car is its own Rail Post Office (RPO) on the rails. There is a catch hook on the side of this car that picks up mail along the railway. Today, just as their catch hook picked up a bag in Port Clinton, along Lake Erie, Owney began seriously sniffing that gray mail pouch. Then he began barking, first at no one, then at Ralph, the RPO clerk from Albany. Owney wouldn't stop barking until Ralph came over and asked Owney what he was doing.

Owney barked at the bag and then at Ralph. Then he nosed the bag. What could be inside?

ALBANY

Finally, Ralph noticed that the pouch label with the city post office address where this bag was going had been improperly attached. What was this? A small mistake or a big mystery?

Ralph called Supervisor Henry over and he opened the bag. Inside, he found a small wiggling bundle with an address tag on it. He un-wrapped the bundle and found a golden puppy dog. Owney yelped and Ralph gulped.

Owney picked up the small pup by the scruff of her neck, and dragged her over to his saucer of milk, always right there beside the stacking machine. Owney kept nosing the pup toward the milk until the pup got the idea--lap up some milk.

Supervisor Henry went up to tell the conductor to wire ahead and tell the Chicago Postal Supervisor to be ready to have the Grand Central Station nurse take the pup and find a home for her. Then, Supervisor Henry and Ralph looked at Owney and wondered how he had known about the pup.

"Ya, know, Ralph, Owney there saved that pup's life."

GENERAL UNION PASSENGER DEPOT OF CHICAGO & ALTON RAILROA
CORNER MADISON AND CANAL STREETS, CHICAGO.

ILLINOIS CENTRAL TRAIN STATION

70090 DEARBORN STREET STATION, CHICAGO, ILL.

**T**oday Owney is in one of his favorite places. Chicago. There was not just one train station here, there were six. Owney could get off at one train station and take a shuttle to another to ride on trains going from east to west or to north or south. Owney was a Lucky Dog because he traveled anywhere in America where mail trains or wagons went to deliver the mail.

After taking the shuttle wagon from Grand Central Station to Union Station, Owney found a certain mailbag he liked for its smell. Gray like the others, poochy like the others, filled with letters just like the one from which he had nosed out the golden pup. But this bag was different from the others for its smell.

Owney just could not part with this mailbag, yet he didn't know the mail pouch label read: California letters/Chicago Council Bluffs RPO (which meant that he would go also to Omaha RPO, Ogden RPO, Oakland RPO, and then on to Cloverdale, Calif.)

These were all faraway western places. This could be a big trip!

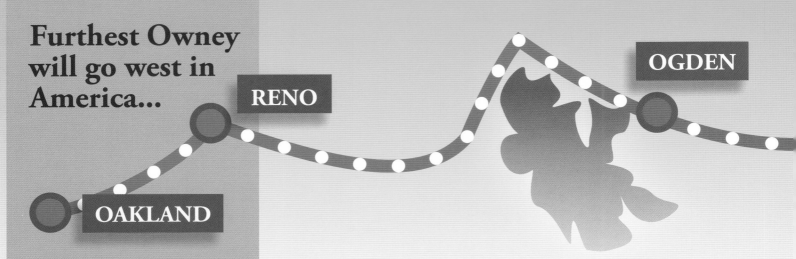

## Furthest Owney will go west in America...

**OGDEN**

**RENO**

**OAKLAND**

It is a long long ride from Chicago to Council Bluffs and Omaha on the Burlington Railroad. There will be plenty of time for good naps on this special smelly poochy bag bound for Cloverdale, California, wherever that is.

While Owney napped, clerks opened gray bags and sorted the mail into a wall rack with "pigeon holes" and then tied them with twine and put them into other bags. At Council Bluffs, Iowa, a friendly clerk motioned the Union Pacific RR westbound mail wagon forward to meet the inbound Burlington train. The Union Pacific train would travel across the Missouri River to Omaha and then head for Ogden, Utah. Owney climbed aboard, following his favorite gray bag.

Moving across the Rocky Mountains, Owney enjoyed the new smells of the flowers and trees, all kinds of trees. He barked at the wind as the spirit of coming attractions began to show him this was going to be a very special journey.

At the big station in Ogden, Owney changed to the RPO car of the Southern Pacific Railroad bound for Oakland, California. Never was his smelly poochy bag away from him.

A short time from Ogden, Howard, the postal worker, tapped Owney and said, "Hey, little friend, come on over here. I'm going to open the door here so you can see and smell out to the Lake."

The blowing smell of the Great Salt Lake filled the postal car with a great salty breeze. Owney took a big sniff and looked out the door to the passing Lake. Boy, was it big. "That there is Salt Lake. You wouldn't want to fall into that one, nor would you want to lick it up. It's all salt and water out here in the middle of the Utah desert." Owney's sense of adventure had been right--this was a special trip for a dog.

CHICAGO

COUNCIL BLUFFS
OMAHA

At Reno, Nevada, the RPO crew was joined by men in blue uniforms with guns. They were guards and they helped the RPO workers to load bags, many white bags that were small and heavy onto the train. Owney knew they were heavy because the postal crew struggled to carry them. What were they?

A man in a blue uniform counted the white bags carefully and made notes to be sure they were all accounted for. Joe Two, the new RPO man from Reno saw the dog and said, "Hey, you're Owney! I heard about you! How come you never been to Reno before? Aw, I bet you've never seen bags of silver dollars. Some pile o' hard cash, huh? Hundred dollars a bag, melted up just south o' here in Carson City where the government has a real mint to make money. Boy, I wish I could get a bag o' them. None of that paper money for me--give me cold hard cash."

Owney kept trying to find their scent. Everything had smell, but these didn't. All the way to Oakland, Owney went from his own poochy bag to these strange bags with no smell. How could that be?

Then the train arrived in Oakland California and there was more water than Owney had ever seen --- the San Francisco Bay and the Pacific Ocean.

**B**ack by the lake of salt, Owney's train had to travel around the water. Now he would get to go over the water of San Francisco Bay on the ferry boat to Ferry House, where Owney and the mail bags, including the mysterious white bags filled with silver dollars, would travel on the railroad streetcar to drop off the coins at the Mint. Then they would travel on to the tip of San Francisco.

There was a water gap between where the railroad streetcar stopped and where they needed to go across the Bay to Sausalito and then north to Cloverdale. But now Owney could fill his nose with the sweet scents of the Pacific Ocean. He couldn't even see across to the other side. Well, maybe someday . . .

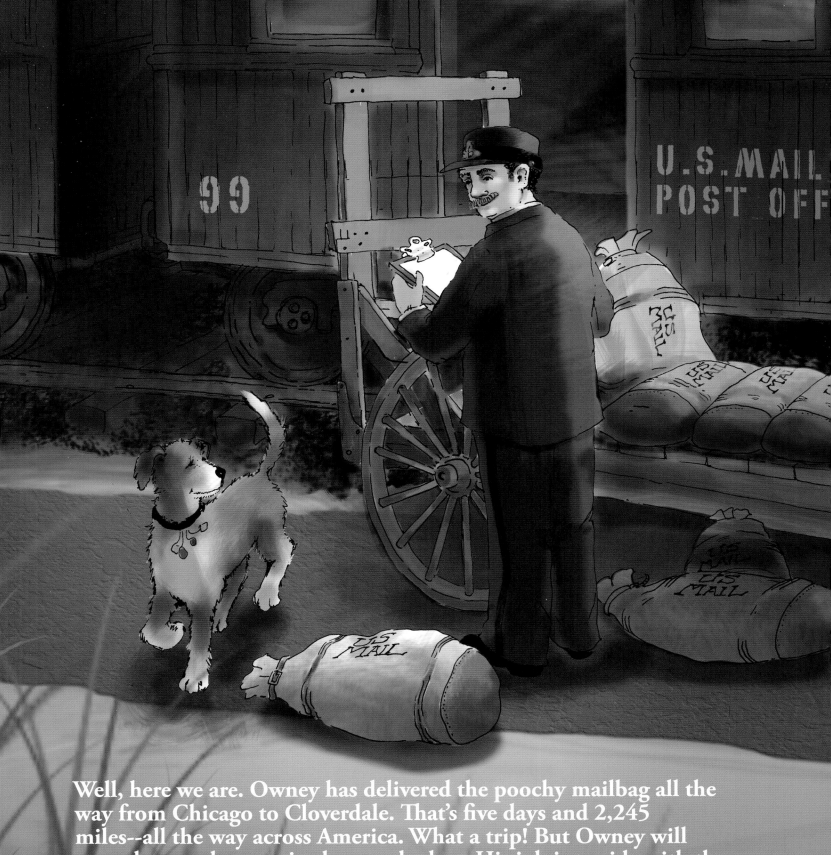

Well, here we are. Owney has delivered the poochy mailbag all the way from Chicago to Cloverdale. That's five days and 2,245 miles--all the way across America. What a trip! But Owney will never know what was in the poochy bag. His job is to ride with the mail, not to open it.

Now, curious, Owney jumps off the mail car to investigate the new sights and smells of Cloverdale. It's different, it's west . . .

Burton, the rail mail man, says to Owney, "Hey, pooch, its only a while we'll be here. Don' wander off too far!"

rom one of the surrounding homes comes a girl dressed prim and proper, as if she is going to a birthday party. She walks directly to Owney and kneels down to pet him. Owney has never seen such a fine young lady. Her name is Prim Sarah.

Sarah and Owney begin to play together. She takes Owney to her home and shows her new playmate to her mother, who is delighted to meet this friendly dog. Mom gives Owney food scraps from the last meal and notices the tag on the dog's collar. She reads it to Sarah.

"It says his name is Owney and he lives in the post office in Albany." "Where is Al-bany, Mom?" "Well, hon, it's a faraway place in New York." "That's a long way for this dog--for Owney to travel."

Sarah gets her favorite book and takes Owney out to the porch and begins to read to him.

But before Sarah can reach the end of the story, Owney hears a voice from the train calling him. "Com'on Owney, we goin' back to Albany."

Prim Sarah and Owney hug and whisper to each other. Owney runs off to his life on the trains. Sarah stays behind, shedding a small tear. The train leaves Cloverdale.

n the kitchen of Prim Sarah's small house in Cloverdale the following week, Sarah says to her mother that she loves the dog and misses him. She would like to write him a letter.

e," says her mother, who goes to the desk and produces an elope, a stamp, and a pencil for Sarah, who writes her letter and n puts it into the envelope. Mom carefully writes Owney's name address on the envelope and then lets Sarah lick the stamp and the envelope.

y send the letter to Albany on the next train from Cloverdale.

Owney was so excited to get a letter. He had seen letters for others for years, but had never gotten a letter of his own.

Now, from all over the post office in Albany, Owney hears the voices of the postal workers calling,
   "Owney's got a girlfriend."
   "Owney's got a girlfriend . . ."

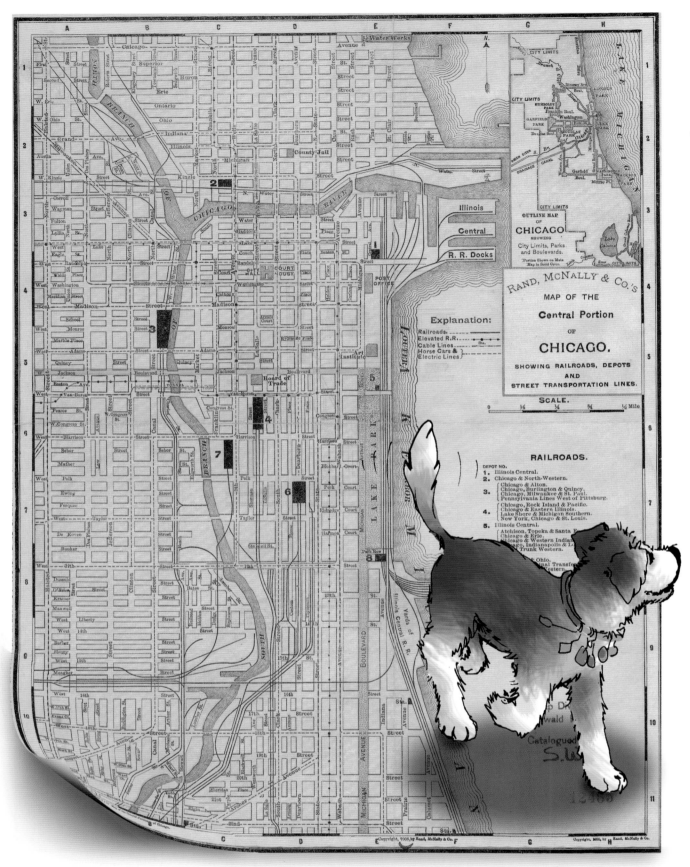

**T**oday Owney finds himself again in Chicago, so he hops a mail transfer train riding from the heart of Chicago to its South Side and the Illinois Central Station, which is where everyone gets off to go to the Fair.

What Fair? wonders Owney.

Owney just followed the crowd. He could always go any-where, but this was different: the Fair was bigger than a train station, and nicer, with bushes and lawns and interesting places to sniff. This looked like a good adventure. Maybe he would meet some new friends!

WORLD'S COLUMBIAN EXPOSITION

O h, boy, thought Owney, so this is what a Fair is. What a fine place. And this family seems nice.

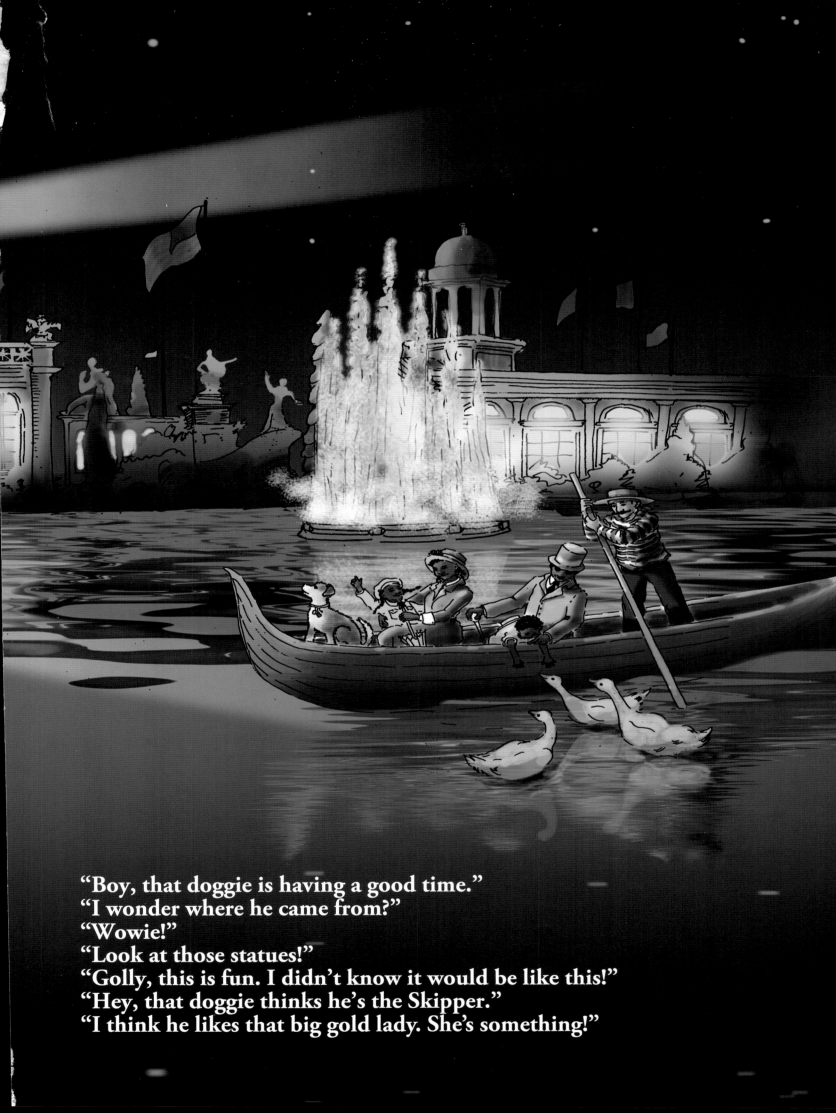

"Boy, that doggie is having a good time."
"I wonder where he came from?"
"Wowie!"
"Look at those statues!"
"Golly, this is fun. I didn't know it would be like this!"
"Hey, that doggie thinks he's the Skipper."
"I think he likes that big gold lady. She's something!"

**O**wney looked up at the largest round thing he had ever seen. What could that be? Then a big man with white hair walked up to him. "Hullo, Pooch. Some big wheel, eh?" The big man with the white hair reached down to look at Owney's tag. "Owney, from Albany, eh? Well, fine, Owney, my name is Tom Edison and I am from New Jersey." Owney stood on his hind legs and wagged his tail at the big man.

Then the man said, "Want to take a ride on Mr. Ferris's Wheel?" Owney barked at the big man. Mr. Edison explained to Owney that this was the first Ferris Wheel to be shown anywhere. That's what World's Fairs were for, he said, to show off inventions.

Mr. Edison was kindly and no one had ever talked so much to Owney.
It was as if Owney was a regular person. What Owney didn't know
was that Mr. Edison was at the Fair because he was a fine inventor,
and at this Fair, he was
introducing the first
motion picture film
player. Mr. Edison
called it a Kinetoscope.
A person could look
into the eyepiece of this
Kinetoscope and press a
button and see "motion
pictures". Tom was pleased that his new
invention was a big hit at the World's
Fair in 1893.

**B**efore you could say "whiz bang," Owney and Tom Edison were up in that wheel, at the top, looking out the window over the whole Fair--my, how big and grand it was! A person and a dog could see all the way to Lake Michigan. What a thrill and what a sight . . . and the gondolas on the Wheel rocked, too.

In all his travels Owney had never been to a place like the World's Fair. People at the Fair were good to dogs, and now he was friends with the big white-haired man.

CHEYENNE

When the ride was over, Mr. Edison patted Owney and said good-bye and that he hoped they would meet again. For Owney, it was time to get back to the trains. As luck or the train schedule would have it, the train he got on was headed west. So it was late at night when Owney's train pulled into Cheyenne, Wyoming. This would be the last stop for the day.

The nice RPO worker jumped off the train and called for Owney to come with him. They stepped across the many tracks and went through the train station. They came out the other side of the station to the main street of Cheyenne, which was dark and seemed abandoned. The postal worker and Owney walked along the main street to the lighted sign of the Wyoming Hotel.

O wney and the postal worker have done this in many towns, so they know there can be different outcomes inside the hotel. Sometimes the hotel clerk will not know Owney, or not understand that Owney is a well-traveled dog. Then, the postal worker will have to explain who Owney is and why he needs to stay at the hotel.

But this time Owney was treated like a visiting relative. Of course,

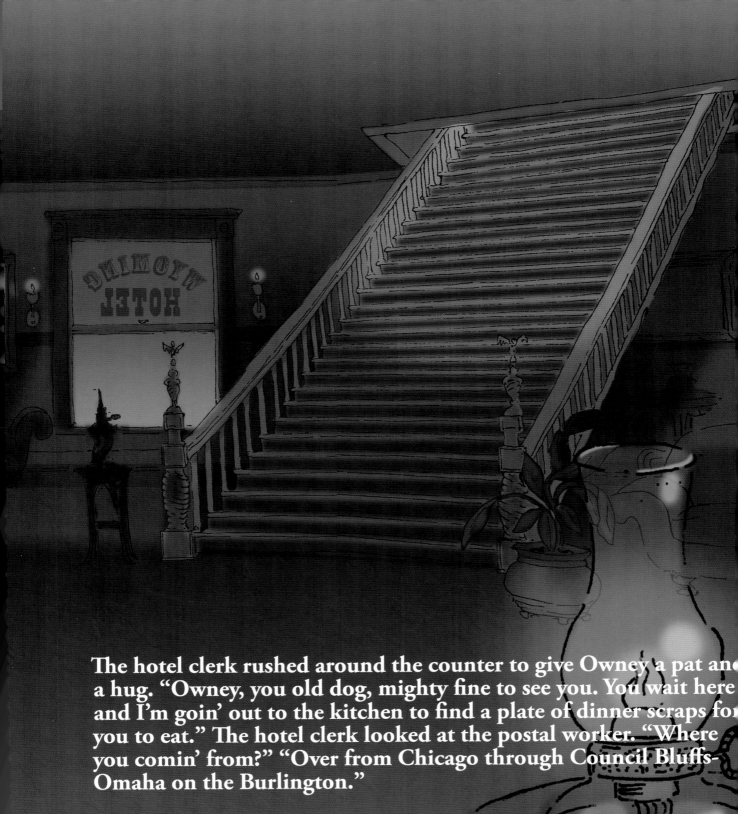

The hotel clerk rushed around the counter to give Owney a pat and a hug. "Owney, you old dog, mighty fine to see you. You wait here and I'm goin' out to the kitchen to find a plate of dinner scraps for you to eat." The hotel clerk looked at the postal worker. "Where you comin' from?" "Over from Chicago through Council Bluffs-Omaha on the Burlington."

The hotel clerk rushed back into the lobby with a plate of food. It looked so good that the postal worker wished he could have some too, but he thanked the man for his kindness and returned to the train. "See ya in the mornin', Owney."

The hotel man patted Owney and said "Glad to see ya back, Owney." After Owney ate, the clerk went upstairs, turning out the lights. Looking at Owney, he said, "'Night, Owney. Don't do

I t is quiet and dark.

The front door of the hotel lobby opens and a young woman enters. She is pretty, about 17 years old, and dressed to travel. She shivers from the night cold. She walks into the middle of the lobby and looks around. She sets down her small bag. As her eyes become adjusted to the dark, she sees the sofa, but not Owney. She walks over and sits.

Owney yelps as she sits on him. They both jump up, scared. Finally, they see each other, woman and dog, and settle down. She sits on the sofa beside Owney and pets him and tells him she's sorry and it's all right, she won't hurt him. She needs a place to stay tonight before the train leaves in the morning. They settle down together on the sofa and Owney licks her hand.

As the young girl falls asleep, she talks, as much to herself as to Owney. He listens while she mumbles about how her folks died and she had to live with her aunt and uncle who are so mean to her that her teeth hurt. She "had to leave," she keeps saying over and over until she falls asleep.

Owney lies with her. She smells right to him. She is not like those gray mailbags, she is soft and warm. He likes that. He doesn't remember ever sleeping with a person before, but he likes sleeping next to her.

I n the morning, as the early sun reached the sofa in the lobby, the young girl woke up and looked at the clock on the wall. She rose up, looked at herself in her small mirror, ran a comb through her hair, and patted her bag. She gently put her hand on Owney to wake him.

"Com' on, little friend . . . wish I knew your name . . . but you are going on the train with me. I need some company on the way to Chicago and maybe we can have some fun together while we are away from here. Honestly, I hope I never have to come back to this place."

The two of them crossed the street and went into the train station. She bought a one-way ticket to Chicago and then headed for the passenger cars. Owney was pleased. He had never been in a passenger car. What a treat! The girl smelled good again this morning. Maybe she was all right to be with--to be his new friend. But would they wonder in the mail car where he was?

Back at the hotel, the clerk comes downstairs. The dog is gone! Where? He looks everywhere but no Owney. He runs across the street to the train and finds the postal worker who is getting ready to come for Owney. The postal worker is horrified. Owney can't be gone! He is so dependable! What would everyone in Albany say if he came home empty-handed!! No Owney??? Not possible. They search everywhere, but Owney is not to be found.

They are trying to decide what to do when the conductor of the train finds them and says, "Owney is up in the passenger compartment with a young woman, who says he belongs to her."

**W**ell, this is new for Owney. Here he sits on the soft red seats with his new friend, Carrie. This is nicer than the mail car. There are fresh smells and the young woman is kind and has already gotten him a pan of water. Where did she get that? This is all right. It seems like a good way to get back to Chicago and Albany.

Owney and Carrie sit and wait patiently for the train to leave Cheyenne.

There wasn't any trouble in Chicago when Owney arrived with Carrie from Cheyenne. The postal worker came up into the passenger car and told her who Owney was, and that both Owney and he had to return to their home station in Albany. He hoped she would understand, and that she would have a good life in Chicago.

Carrie kissed Owney good-bye with a tear in her eye. He liked her, too. She seemed to care for him, she smelled good, and she was a lot softer than the gray mailbags. He was sorry to leave her, but "home station" was Albany.

**A**s always for Owney, it was good to be home. Even a travelin' dog needs the comfort of old friends.

But, there was always those main questions: Where's next and What's next --- new adventures and maybe some new friends?

**I**magine a dog, a plain ordinary, everyday mutt, who finds himself taken into a U.S. post office and is allowed to live there for nine years--from 1887 to 1896. Yet, this was a real dog who lived a real life and became the legendary postal mascot during this period, so legendary that he now "lives" in the Smithsonian Postal Museum in Washington, D.C.

*A Lucky Dog* is our first book about Owney's life.

The historical good luck of Owney's story is that after he died, in 1896, he left a large number of "bagging tags" that were attached to his collar each time he visited a city or a post office. These tags allow us to know the truth about Owney's travels, an approximation of how many places he visited. His tags and honors show us how he made many friends as he traveled.

What we don't know about Owney, is exactly where he went on each trip and exactly who he met. The amazing part of his story is that he traveled to all these places alone. He rode on any train he wanted from city to city, and on any mail wagon within any city. What this tells us, along with what we know as fact, is that Owney had a life, friends, and adventures that were not recorded. To accept and understand that is one of the important meanings of Owney's life: he lived in a different, more generous, easier world. In a way, he is here to "tell us" about this past world.

This book attempts to expand on factual history to tell a wider story of his life, his friends, and his adventures--out of the possibilities of who he might have met and where he might have gone, or, what we might know about him if one of us had traveled along with him, out of sight, watching this remarkable dog make friends and have adventures none of us could even dream of.

One of the factual matters that this book considers was the importance of Chicago as a central railhead for cross-country train travel during this period. To have adventures across the county, Owney could not avoid, factually, moving often through Chicago. That would not only be fun for him, but also allow him opportunities to take advantage of the many attractions in Chicago during that period, like the World Columbian Exposition of 1893, or what is referred to now as the White City. If the people of that world stopped in Chicago and visited the Fair, why not Owney?

This is the expansion of Owney's story. A story sprinkled with facts as well as things that might have been.

Dirk Wales

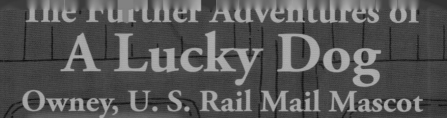

# The Further Adventures of
# A Lucky Dog
## Owney, U. S. Rail Mail Mascot

· · · · · · · · · · · · · · · · · · · · · · · · · · · ·

Written by Dirk Wales

Illustrated by Catherine DeJong Artman
and Townsend Artman

· · · · · · · · · · · · · · · · · · · · · · · · · · · ·

We would like to recognize those who have
helped to make this book as true and factual as possible:
Frank Scheer
Curator – Railway Mail Service Library
We would like to honor the memory of
Virginia Bowers,
Historian of the City of Albany
who passed away in 2008
We'd like to give special thanks to
Hazel E. Robinson, Vintage Postcards
Chris Winters, Bibliographer for Anthropology, Geography and Maps,
University of Chicago
Numismatic Guaranty Corporation
University of Maryland, University Libraries
…and, those who keep Owney safe
at the Smithsonian National Postal Museum

GREAT PLAINS PRESS

©2009
Great Plains Press
2532 West Warren Blvd.
Chicago, Illinois 60612
Phone: 312.850.0373  Fax: 312.850.1274

www.greatplainspress.com

ISBN# 978-0-9632459-6-0

Printed in China

10 9 8 7 6 5 4 3 2 1